A Gift For: _____

From: _____

Editorial Strategist: Delia Berrigan
Editors: Chelsea Resnick and Kim Schworm Acosta
Art Director: Chris Opheim
Designer/Production Designer: Dan Horton

ISBN: 978-1-63059-894-5
BOK9906
Made in China

0517

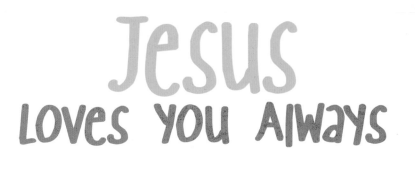

BOOK 1

Jesus
Loves You Always

By Korynn Freels

Illustrated by Kathryn Selbert

There's something very wonderful
that everyone should know—
Jesus loves children just like you,
the Bible says it's so!

One day, believers took their kids
to Jesus to be blessed.
His helpers didn't think that kids
belonged among the rest.

"The Lord does not have time for kids.
Go on now. Move along."

But Jesus stopped their shooing off
and showed them they were wrong!

He told all of His helpers,
"Let the children come to me!"
He welcomed them into His arms
for everyone to see.

He knew kids have a special way
of helping grown-ups, too.
They teach important lessons
in the things they say and do.

Kids see the good and have big hearts.
They trust and care with ease.
God's kingdom, Jesus told the world,
"belongs to such as these!"

He taught all of His helpers,
"Welcome children in My name.
And every time you welcome kids,
you welcome God the same!"

Jesus shared God's words of love
traveling far and wide.

Every place the good Lord went,
He called kids to His side.

Yes, Jesus cares so very much
for children everywhere—
their laughter, hugs, and happy smiles,
and all the joy they share.

So know that Jesus loves you!
And in all you say and do,
you make God's world a happy place
by simply being you.

Did you enjoy this book?
We'd love to hear from you!

Please send your comments to:
Hallmark Book Feedback
P.O. Box 419034
Mail Drop 100
Kansas City, MO 64141

Or e-mail us at:
booknotes@hallmark.com